FIRST DAY Of 2nd GRADE

Written By: Natalie Brown

Illustrated By: Zara Malik

1

ACKNOWLEDGEMENTS

I would like to thank God first for giving me the creativity to come up with stories off the top of my head to bring enjoyment to my son and any child reading this book.

I would also like to thank my husband for encouraging me to turn the nighttime stories I made up for our son into books.

Lastly, I would like to thank my son for being the inspiration for these stories and specifically Thomas in these stories, without you there would be no stories to tell.

CHARACTER VOICE DESCRIPTION

When telling this story to my son I would use different voices for the characters to make the story more interesting and come to life. Below is a description of the characters and their voices so when you read the book, if you choose to, you can use different voices for the characters too.

Thomas: I used my regular voice but more child like

Thomas's Mom: I used my regular voice

Billy Bob: I talked really country

Tutu Putt: I talked like I was from India

Molly: I used a bubbly, high energy voice

Sally: I used a more laid-back voice.

It was Thomas's first day of 2nd grade and he was excited and a little nervous at the same time. Thomas has his backpack on and is ready to go to school, he asked, "mom what if I don't make any friends?" "I'm sure you will," his mom replied.

Thomas was sitting in the gym at school waiting for class to start and he felt a tap on his shoulder. "Hello, my name is Billy Bob, what's your name?" "My name is Thomas." "Nice to meet you," said Billy Bob.

"Just in case you want to know me better, I'm a country boy. I like to fish, hunt, wear overalls and ride in pickup trucks, what do you like to do?" asked Billy Bob.

"I like to read," said Thomas.

"Alright," what else do you like to do?

asked Billy Bob.

"I like to play video games!" exclaimed Thomas. "Really, you are too young, video games aren't good for you at this age," said Billy Bob. "What else do you like to do?" asked Billy Bob.

"I like to play basketball," Thomas said. "Now you're talking, that's fun and I like to play too, maybe we can play sometime," said Billy Bob.

"Who is your teacher?" asked Billy Bob. "Mrs. Jacobs," said Thomas. "I have Mrs. Jacobs too, I am so excited, we are going to be the best of friends!" Billy Bob exclaimed.

Billy Bob got to class before Thomas.

"Sit by me," said Billy Bob.

Another boy sat on Thomas's left. "What's your name?" asked Thomas. "My name is Tutu Putt" "Where you from?" asked Billy Bob. "I'm from India, my parents moved to the United States when I was just a little baby, "said Tutu. "Welcome to America!" exclaimed Billy Bob.

Just then another student walks in the class. "I am so excited to be here and see all you wonderful people!" exclaimed Molly. "My name is Molly." Molly introduced herself to Thomas, Billy Bob and Tutu Putt. "It is so nice to meet you all, don't you just love my little pony shirt, I love my little pony!" Molly exclaimed.

Another new girl came in the class and Molly yelled, "Sit by me, sit by me!" "What's your name?" asked Molly. "My name is Sally" "Nice to meet you, my name is Molly." "What do you like to do for fun?" asked Molly. "I like to go shopping for clothes and dolls," Sally said. "I like to go shopping too, maybe we can go together some time with our parents and I can buy some more my little ponies," said Molly. "Sounds like fun," Sally replied.

"Hey everybody, it would be so awesome if we could all sit together for lunch!" exclaimed Molly. "I think we will all be sitting together for lunch because we are all in the same class," replied Billy Bob.

They all ended up sitting together at lunch and got to know each other better. This would be the first day of friendships that would last through the years.

ABOUT THE AUTHOR

Natalie Brown resides in Georgia with her Husband Danny and Son Morgan. She is a new author, and this is her first book in a series of books about Thomas. Her son Morgan was the inspiration for Thomas. These stories came about as bedtime stories she would tell her son that she would make up off the top of her head. These stories started when her son was six years old, he is eleven years old today and still requests a Thomas story before he goes to bed.

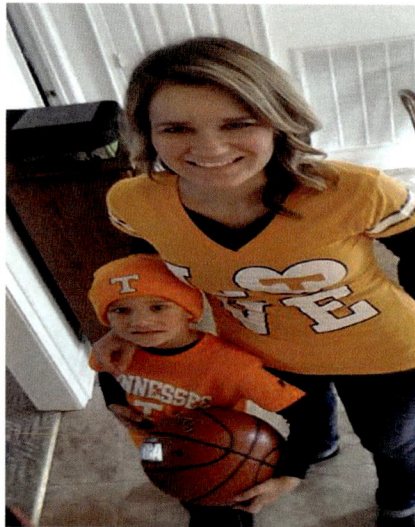

First Day of 2nd Grade Review

If you enjoyed this book, I'd like to hear from you and hope that you could take some time to post a review on Amazon. Your feedback and support are important to me and really helps a new author like myself.

You can go into where you purchased the book, and it gives you an option to leave a review or you can follow this link https://a.co/d/cO001if scroll down the page and you will see where to leave a review.

Or use http://www.amazon.com/review/create-review?&asin=B0BYH3X7F6

Also, if you could share on any social media account you might have facebook or twitter I would appreciate it.

Other Books from Natalie Brown

God Inspired Poems of My Life

Available on Amazon

Made in the USA
Las Vegas, NV
08 July 2025